Author: Callie Chapman
Illustrator: Bronwyne Chapman & Callie Chapman
Printing: www.artbookbindery.com

ISBN 0-9973968-5-0

Check out the entire award winning Glitter the Unicorn series,
Glitter the Unicorn, Glitter The Unicorn Goes to the Beach and
Glitter the Unicorn Goes to the Moon.
Be on the look out for more Glitter the Unicorn adventures.
www.glittertheunicorn.com

Glitter The Unicorn

Goes to the Beach

By Callie Chapman

Seven-year-old Callie lives in Alabama with her family. This imaginative, smart, and funny girl came up with the story of Glitter the Unicorn and her best friend Ellie, named after her favorite stuffed animals. "Glitter the Unicorn Goes to the Beach" is the second book written by Callie regarding the adventures of Glitter the Unicorn and Ellie. Callie loves creating stories..so be on the look out for more adventures for Glitter the Unicorn.

One Morning,
Glitter the Unicorn and Ellie
went to the beach.

Glitter and Ellie were playing with their favorite... Bounce Ball.

The
BALL BOUNCED
into the ocean.

A
Mermaid Queen
took the bounce ball.
Glitter and Ellie were SAD.

A princess Mermaid
swam up to
Glitter and ...

turned
Glitter the Unicorn
into a **Sea Horse**

and ELLie into a
mermaid.

Glitter and **ELLie** followed the princess through the **Cave of Crystals.**

The crystals were all the colors of the rainbow. ELLie twisted a crystal and a colorful piece broke off into her hand.

Glitter and Ellie
kept swimming
until they saw
the Queen's castle.

There were
Turtle Guards
guarding the castle.

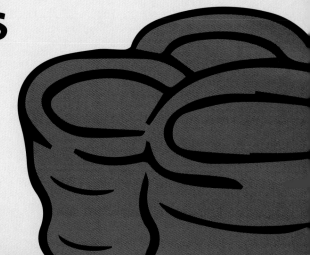

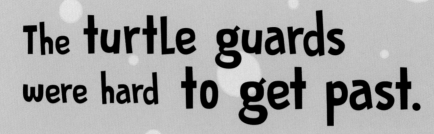

The **turtle guards**
were hard **to get past.**

ELLie and GLitter
tricked
the guards
by GLitter swimming up
and ELLie swimming down.

After getting past the turtle guards, Glitter and Ellie saw an **Octopus.**

The Octopus was dancing. Glitter and Ellie slid under his arms.

Glitter and Ellie followed the Princess into the sea castle.

Glitter and Ellie then saw the Queen with their Bounce Ball.

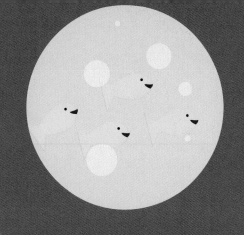

Glitter and Ellie asked the
Queen Mermaid for their
Bounce Ball back.

The Queen said,
"Only on one condition
will I give you your
Bounce Ball.

I will
trade your
Bounce Ball
for the magical crystal."

So, Glitter and Ellie **gave** the Queen Mermaid the crystal for her **crown.**

Pow!!
GLitter turned
back into a
Unicorn and ELLie
turned back to herself.

Glitter the Unicorn and Ellie swam back to the beach.

They played with the **BOUNCE BALL** and built sandcastles.

Glitter and Ellie
went back home...
Glitter Looked up to the sky and said,

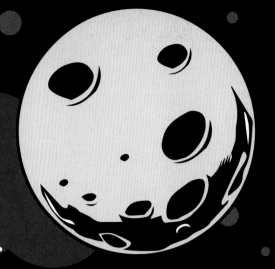

"Let's go to
the MOON!"

The End.